The Reluctant Dragon

Kenneth Grahame
Adapted by Katie Daynes

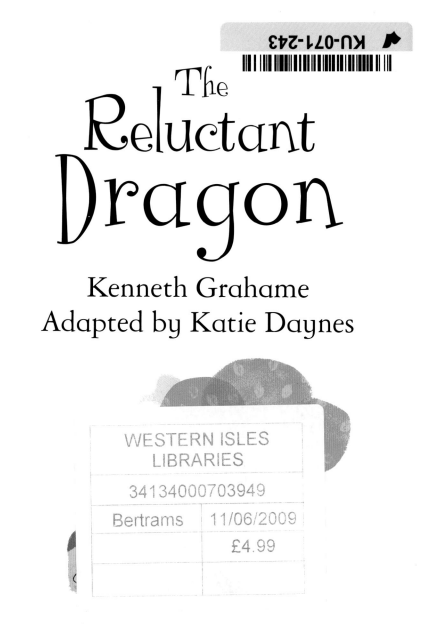

Illustrated by Fred Blunt

Reading Consultant: Alison Kelly
Roehampton University

One evening,
long ago, a shepherd
ran home, terrified.

"I saw something terrible," he cried to his wife and son.

It's as big as four horses!

"It has long,
sharp claws...

a long, pointy
tail...

...and shiny blue
scales all over
its body."

His son looked up
from his book.

"That sounds like a
dragon," he said.

"A dragon?" yelped the wife.

"A *dragon*?" said the shepherd.

"That does not sound good."

The boy wasn't
scared. The next day,
he set off up the hill
to find the
dragon.

Bye. Don't
worry!

"He might be friendly,"
thought the boy.

The dragon *was*
friendly – and he was
thrilled to see the boy.

It's beautiful
here, but it does
get lonely.

10

The boy smiled. He sat
down and asked the dragon
all kinds of questions.

The dragon told stories of long, long ago.

There were dangerous dragons everywhere.

And brave knights fought
them to rescue princesses.

The boy came back every
day to hear the stories.

But then the villagers found
out about the dragon. They
were terrified.

The boy ran straight to the dragon. "The villagers want to get rid of you!" he panted.

But I wouldn't hurt a fly!

That afternoon, the boy
heard even worse news.

He's here!

Who's here?

Saint George, the Dragon Killer!

He's going to fight the dragon!

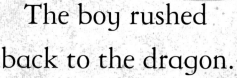

The boy rushed back to the dragon.

"Saint George the Dragon Killer wants to fight you," gasped the boy.

"And he has the longest spear I've ever seen."

But I don't like fighting.

"I'll just hide in my cave until he goes away," said the dragon.

"You can't!" cried the boy. "Everyone wants a fight!"

The dragon yawned.
"I'm sure you'll think of
something," he said.

The boy walked slowly
back down to the village.

He eats ten sheep
for breakfast.

A crowd of villagers
was telling George about
the dangerous dragon.

He burned
down five
houses.

"It's not true!" said the boy.
"The dragon wouldn't hurt
a fly."

"But everyone wants a fight," said George. "What can I do?"

"Follow me," said the boy. And he took George to meet the dragon.

"What a perfect place for a fight," said George.

"No fighting," said the dragon, firmly.

"Not even a
pretend fight?"
asked the boy.

"Maybe..."
said the dragon.

27

The boy turned to George.
"Do you promise not to
hurt him?"

"Well, it has to look
real," said George.

"Will there be a feast
afterwards?" asked
the dragon.

"There will, and you can
come," promised George.

The next morning,
lots of villagers
arrived to watch
the fight.

The boy waited
nervously by the
dragon's cave.

They cheered and waved
when Saint George rode into
view. But where was the
dragon?

Then a roar echoed around
the hills. Flames filled
the air.

Everyone gasped as the dragon appeared. His scales sparkled and he breathed out fire.

"Charge!" cried George.
He galloped hard, his spear
held high.

The dragon bounded up.

And they shot past each other.

"Missed!" yelled the crowd.

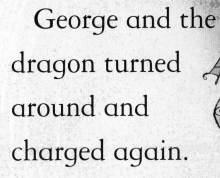

George and the dragon turned around and charged again.

37

This time, there was no
way they could miss.
CLATTER! BANG! OUF!

The dragon slumped to the ground. George towered over him.

Cut off his head!

"I think the dragon
has learned his lesson," George
declared. "Let's invite him
to our feast."

And he led the villagers,
the boy and the dragon back
down the hill.

The boy was happy
because his plan worked.

The villagers were
happy because they'd seen
a fight. George was happy
because he'd won.

The dragon was happiest
of all. He had lots of
new friends...

...and a very
full tummy.

"Jolly night it's been,"
he murmured and
began to snore.

"How will I get him
home?" said the boy.

"I'll help," said George.
He gave the dragon a prod.

45

And they set off up the
hill arm-in-arm — the saint,
the dragon and the boy.

About this story

The Reluctant Dragon was first
published over 100 years
ago. The author,
Kenneth Grahame,
also wrote
the famous
children's story
*The Wind in
the Willows.*

Designed by Caroline Spatz
Digital manipulation: John Russell
Series editor: Lesley Sims
Series designer: Russell Punter

First published in 2009 by Usborne Publishing Ltd., Usborne House,
83-85 Saffron Hill, London EC1N 8RT, England. www.usborne.com
Copyright © 2009 Usborne Publishing Ltd.

USBORNE FIRST READING
Level Four

USBORNE FIRST READING

Baba Yaga
The Flying Witch

Susanna Davidson
Illustrated by
Sara Rojo

USBORNE FIRST READING

Butterflies

Kate Davies
Illustrated by Jana Costa

USBORNE FIRST READING

Dick Whittington

London 10 miles

Retold by
Russell Punter
Illustrated by
Barbara Vagnozzi

USBORNE FIRST READING

Androcles
and the
Lion

Retold by Russell Punter
Illustrated by Mike and Carl Gordon

USBORNE FIRST READING

Goldilocks and
The Three Bears

retold by
Susanna Davidson
Illustrated by Mike Gordon

USBORNE FIRST READING

Penguins

Susanna Davidson
Illustrated by Simon Mendez

USBORNE FIRST READING

Percy
and the
Pirates

Russell Punter
Illustrated by Kate Sheppard

USBORNE FIRST READING

Princess
Polly and the
Pony

Susanna Davidson
Illustrated by Dave Hill

USBORNE FIRST READING

Little Red
Riding Hood

based on the story by The Brothers Grimm
Illustrated by Mike Gordon